The Patagonia

Henry James

16

EasyRead Large

ReadHowYouWant Classics Library

TABLE OF CONTENTS

CHAPTER I

The houses were dark in the August night and the perspective of Beacon Street, with its double chain of lamps, was a foreshortened desert. The club on the hill alone, from its semi-cylindrical front, projected a glow upon the dusky vagueness of the Common, and as I passed it I heard in the hot stillness the click of a pair of billiard-balls. As "every one" was out of town perhaps the servants, in the extravagance of their leisure, were profaning the tables. The heat was insufferable and I thought with joy of the morrow, of the deck of the steamer, the freshening breeze, the sense of getting out to sea. I was even glad of what I had learned in the afternoon at the office of the company – that at the eleventh hour an old ship with a lower standard of speed had been put on in place of the vessel in which I had taken my passage. America was roasting, England might very well be stuffy, and a slow passage (which at that season of the year would probably also be a fine one) was a guarantee of ten or twelve days of fresh air.

I strolled down the hill without meeting a creature, though I could see through the palings of the Common that that recreative expanse was peopled with dim forms. I remembered Mrs. Nettlepoint's house – she lived in those days (they are not so distant, but there have been changes) on the waterside, a little way beyond the spot at which the Public Garden terminates; and I reflected that like myself she would be spending the night in Boston if it were true that, as had been mentioned to me a few days before at Mount Desert, she was to embark on the morrow for Liverpool. I presently saw this appearance confirmed by a light above her door and in two or three of her windows, and I determined to ask for her, having nothing to do till bedtime. I had come out simply to pass an hour, leaving my hotel to the blaze of its gas and the perspiration of its porters; but it occurred to me that my old friend might very WELL not know of the substitution of the Patagonia for the Scandinavia, so that I should be doing her a service to prepare her mind. Besides, I could offer to help her, to look after her in the morning: lone women are grateful for support in taking ship for far countries.

It came to me indeed as I stood on her doorstep that as she had a son she might not after all be so lone; yet I remembered at the same time that Jasper Nettlepoint was not quite a young man to lean upon, having – as I at least supposed – a life of his own and tastes and habits which had long since diverted him from the maternal side. If he did happen just now to be at home my solicitude would of course seem officious; for in his many wanderings – I believed he had roamed all over the globe – he would certainly have learned how to manage. None the less, in fine, I was very glad to show Mrs. Nettlepoint I thought of her. With my long absence I had lost sight of her; but I had liked her of old, she had been a good friend to my sisters, and I had in regard to her that sense which is pleasant to those who in general have gone astray or got detached, the sense that she at least knew all about me. I could trust her at any time to tell people I was respectable. Perhaps I was conscious of how little I deserved this indulgence when it came over me that I hadn't been near her for ages. The measure of that neglect was given by my vagueness of mind about Jasper. However, I really belonged nowadays to a different generation; I was more the mother's contemporary than the son's.

Mrs. Nettlepoint was at home: I found her in her back drawing-room, where the wide windows opened to the water. The room was dusky – it was too hot for lamps – and she sat slowly moving her fan and looking out on the little arm of the sea which is so pretty at night, reflecting the lights of Cambridgeport and Charlestown. I supposed she was musing on the loved ones she was to leave behind, her married daughters, her grandchildren; but she struck a note more specifically Bostonian as she said to me, pointing with her fan to the Back Bay: "I shall see nothing more charming than that over there, you know!" She made me very welcome, but her son had told her about the Patagonia, for which she was sorry, as this would mean a longer voyage. She was a poor creature in any boat and mainly confined to her cabin even in weather extravagantly termed fine – as if any weather could be fine at sea.

"Ah then your son's going with you?" I asked.

"Here he comes, he'll tell you for himself much better than I can pretend to." Jasper Nettlepoint at that moment joined us, dressed in white flannel and carrying a large fan. "Well, my dear, have you decided?" his mother continued with no scant irony. "He hasn't yet made up his mind, and we sail at ten o'clock!"

"What does it matter when my things are put up?" the young man said. "There's no crowd at this moment; there will be cabins to spare. I'm waiting for a telegram – that will settle it. I just walked up to the club to see if it was come – they'll send it there because they suppose this house unoccupied. Not yet, but I shall go back in twenty minutes."

"Mercy, how you rush about in this temperature!" the poor lady exclaimed while I reflected that it was perhaps HIS billiard-balls I had heard ten minutes before. I was sure he was fond of billiards.

"Rush? not in the least. I take it uncommon easy."

"Ah I'm bound to say you do!" Mrs. Nettlepoint returned with inconsequence. I guessed at a certain tension between the pair and a want of consideration on the young man's part, arising perhaps from selfishness. His mother was nervous, in suspense, wanting to be at rest as to whether she should have his company on the voyage or be obliged to struggle alone. But as he stood there smiling and slowly moving his fan he struck me somehow as a person on whom this fact wouldn't sit too heavily. He was of the type of those whom other people worry about, not of those who worry about other people. Tall and strong, he had a handsome face, with a round head and close-curling hair; the whites of his eyes and the enamel of his teeth, under his brown moustache, gleamed vaguely in the lights of the Back Bay. I made out that he was sunburnt, as if he lived much in the open air, and that he looked intelligent but also slightly brutal, though not in a morose way. His brutality, if he had any, was bright and finished. I had to tell him who I was, but even then I saw how little he placed me and that my explanations gave me in his mind no great identity or at any rate no great importance. I foresaw that he would in intercourse make me feel sometimes very young and sometimes very old, caring himself but little which. He mentioned, as if to show our companion that he might safely be left to his own devices, that he had once started from London to Bombay at three quarters of an hour's notice.

"Yes, and it must have been pleasant for the people you were with!"

"Oh the people I was with–!" he returned; and his tone appeared to signify that such people would always have to come off as they could. He asked if there were no cold drinks in the house, no lemonade, no iced syrups; in such weather something of that sort ought always to be kept going. When his mother remarked that surely at the club they WERE kept going he went on: "Oh yes, I had various things there; but you know I've walked down the hill since. One should have something at either end. May I ring and see?" He rang while Mrs. Nettlepoint observed that with the people they had in the house, an establishment reduced naturally at such a moment to its simplest expression – they were burning up candle-ends and there were no luxuries – she wouldn't answer for the service. The matter ended in her leaving the room in quest of cordials with the female domestic who had arrived in response to the bell and in whom Jasper's appeal aroused no visible intelligence.

She remained away some time and I talked with her son, who was sociable but desultory and kept moving over the place, always with his fan, as if he were properly impatient. Sometimes he seated himself an instant on the windowsill, and then I made him out in fact thoroughly good-looking – a fine brown clean young athlete. He failed to tell me on what special contingency his decision depended; he only alluded familiarly to an expected telegram, and I saw he was probably fond at no time of the trouble of explanations. His mother's absence was a sign that when it might be a question of gratifying him she had grown used to spare no pains, and I fancied her rummaging in some close storeroom, among old preserve-pots, while the dull maidservant held the candle awry. I don't know whether this same vision was in his own eyes; at all events it didn't prevent his saying suddenly, as he looked at his watch, that I must excuse him – he should have to go back to the club. He would return in half an hour – or in less. He walked away and I sat there alone, conscious, on the dark dismantled simplified scene, in the deep silence that rests on American towns during the hot season – there was now and then a far cry or a plash in the water, and at intervals the tinkle of the bells of the horse-cars on the long bridge, slow in the suffocating night – of the strange influence, half-sweet, half-sad, that abides in houses uninhabited or about to become so, in places muffled and bereaved, where the unheeded sofas and patient belittered tables seem (like the disconcerted dogs, to whom everything is alike sinister) to recognise the eve of a journey.

After a while I heard the sound of voices, of steps, the rustle of dresses, and I looked round, supposing these things to denote the return of Mrs. Nettlepoint and her handmaiden with the refection prepared for her son. What I saw however was two other female forms, visitors apparently just admitted, and now ushered into the room. They were not announced – the servant turned her back on them and rambled off to our hostess. They advanced in a wavering tentative unintroduced way – partly, I could see, because the place was dark and partly because their visit was in its nature experimental, a flight of imagination or a stretch of confidence. One of the ladies was stout and the other slim, and I made sure in a moment that one was talkative and the other reserved. It was further to be discerned that one was elderly and the other young, as well as that the fact of their unlikeness didn't prevent their being mother and daughter. Mrs. Nettlepoint reappeared in a very few minutes, but the interval had sufficed to establish a communication – really copious for the occasion – between the strangers and the unknown gentleman whom they found in possession, hat and stick in hand. This was not my doing – for what had I to go upon? – and still less was it the doing of the younger and the more indifferent, or less courageous, lady. She spoke but once – when her companion informed me that she was going out to Europe the next day to be married. Then she protested "Oh mother!" in a tone that struck me in the darkness as doubly odd, exciting my curiosity to see her face.

It had taken the elder woman but a moment to come to that, and to various other things, after I had explained that I myself was waiting for Mrs. Nettlepoint, who would doubtless soon come back.

"Well, she won't know me – I guess she hasn't ever heard much about me," the good lady said; "but I've come from Mrs. Allen and I guess that will make it all right. I presume you know Mrs. Allen?"

I was unacquainted with this influential personage, but I assented vaguely to the proposition. Mrs. Allen's emissary was good-humoured and familiar, but rather appealing than insistent (she remarked that if her friend HAD found time to come in the afternoon – she had so much to do, being just up for the day, that she couldn't be sure – it would be all right); and somehow even before she mentioned Merrimac Avenue (they had come all the way from there) my imagination had associated her with that indefinite social limbo known to the properly-constituted Boston mind as the South End – a nebulous region which condenses here and there into a pretty face, in which the daughters are an "improvement" on the mothers and are sometimes acquainted with gentlemen more gloriously domiciled, gentlemen whose wives and sisters are in turn not acquainted with them.

When at last Mrs. Nettlepoint came in, accompanied by candles and by a tray laden with glasses of coloured fluid which emitted a cool tinkling, I was in a position to officiate as master of the ceremonies, to introduce Mrs. Mavis and Miss Grace Mavis, to represent that Mrs. Allen had recommended them – nay, had urged them – just to come that way, informally and without fear; Mrs. Allen who had been prevented only by the pressure of occupations so characteristic of her (especially when up from Mattapoisett for a few hours' desperate shopping) from herself calling in the course of the day to explain who they were and what was the favour they had to ask of her benevolent friend. Good-natured women understand each other even when so divided as to sit residentially above and below the salt, as who should say; by which token our hostess had quickly mastered the main facts: Mrs. Allen's visit that morning in Merrimac Avenue to talk of Mrs. Amber's great idea, the classes at the public schools in vacation (she was interested with an equal charity to that of Mrs. Mavis – even in such weather! – in those of the South End) for games and exercises and music, to keep the poor unoccupied children out of the streets; then the revelation that it had suddenly been settled almost from one hour to the other that Grace should sail for Liverpool, Mr. Porterfield at last being ready. He was taking a little holiday; his mother was with him, they had come over from Paris to see some of the celebrated old buildings in England, and he had telegraphed to say that if Grace would start right off they would just finish it up and be married. It often happened that when things had dragged on that way for years they were all huddled up at the end. Of course in such a case she, Mrs. Mavis, had had to fly round. Her daughter's passage was taken, but it seemed too dreadful she should make her journey all alone, the first time she had ever been at sea, without any companion or escort. SHE couldn't go – Mr. Mavis was too sick: she hadn't even been able to get him off to the seaside.

"Well, Mrs. Nettlepoint's going in that ship," Mrs. Allen had said; and she had represented that nothing was simpler than to give her the girl in charge. When Mrs. Mavis had replied that this was all very well but that she didn't know the lady, Mrs. Allen had declared that that didn't make a speck of difference, for Mrs. Nettlepoint was kind enough for anything. It was easy enough to KNOW her, if that was all the trouble! All Mrs. Mavis would have to do would be to go right up to her next morning, when she took her daughter to the ship (she would see her there on the deck with her party) and tell her fair and square what she wanted. Mrs. Nettlepoint had daughters herself and would easily understand. Very likely she'd even look after Grace a little on the other side, in such a queer situation, going out alone to the gentleman she was engaged to: she'd just help her, like a good Samaritan, to turn round before she was married. Mr. Porterfield seemed to think they wouldn't wait long, once she was there: they would have it right over at the American consul's. Mrs. Allen had said it would perhaps be better still to go and see Mrs. Nettlepoint beforehand, that day, to tell her what they wanted: then they wouldn't seem to spring it on her just as she was leaving. She herself (Mrs. Allen) would call and say a word for them if she could save ten minutes before catching her train. If she hadn't come it was because she hadn't saved her ten minutes but she had made them feel that they must come all the same. Mrs. Mavis liked that better, because on the ship in the morning there would be such a confusion. She didn't think her daughter would be any trouble – conscientiously she didn't. It was just to have some one to speak to her and not sally forth like a servant-girl going to a situation.

"I see, I'm to act as a sort of bridesmaid and to give her away," Mrs. Nettlepoint obligingly said. Kind enough in fact for anything, she showed on this occasion that it was easy enough to know her. There is notoriously nothing less desirable than an imposed aggravation of effort at sea, but she accepted without betrayed dismay the burden of the young lady's dependence and allowed her, as Mrs. Mavis said, to hook herself on. She evidently had the habit of patience, and her reception of her visitors' story reminded me afresh – I was reminded of it whenever I returned to my native land – that my dear compatriots are the people in the world who most freely take mutual accommodation for granted. They have always had to help themselves, and have rather magnanimously failed to learn just where helping others is distinguishable from that. In no country are there fewer forms and more reciprocities.

It was doubtless not singular that the ladies from Merrimac Avenue shouldn't feel they were importunate: what was striking was that Mrs. Nettlepoint didn't appear to suspect it. However, she would in any case have thought it inhuman to show this – though I could see that under the surface she was amused at everything the more expressive of the pilgrims from the South End took for granted. I scarce know whether the attitude of the younger visitor added or not to the merit of her good nature. Mr. Porterfield's intended took no part in the demonstration, scarcely spoke, sat looking at the Back Bay and the lights on the long bridge. She declined the lemonade and the other mixtures which, at Mrs. Nettlepoint's request, I offered her, while her mother partook freely of everything and I reflected – for I as freely drained a glass or two in which the ice tinkled

– that Mr. Jasper had better hurry back if he wished to enjoy these luxuries.

Was the effect of the young woman's reserve meanwhile ungracious, or was it only natural that in her particular situation she shouldn't have a flow of compliment at her command? I noticed that Mrs. Nettlepoint looked at her often, and certainly though she was undemonstrative Miss Mavis was interesting. The candlelight enabled me to see that though not in the very first flower of her youth she was still fresh and handsome. Her eyes and hair were dark, her face was pale, and she held up her head as if, with its thick braids and everything else involved in it, it were an appurtenance she wasn't ashamed of. If her mother was excellent and common she was not common – not at least flagrantly so – and perhaps also not excellent. At all events she wouldn't be, in appearance at least, a dreary appendage; which in the case of a person "hooking on" was always something gained. Was it because something of a romantic or pathetic interest usually attaches to a good creature who has been the victim of a "long engagement" that this young lady made an impression on me from the first – favoured as I had been so quickly with this glimpse of her history? I could charge her certainly with no positive appeal; she only held her tongue and smiled, and her smile corrected whatever suggestion might have forced itself upon me that the spirit within her was dead – the spirit of that promise of which she found herself doomed to carry out the letter.

What corrected it less, I must add, was an odd recollection which gathered vividness as I listened to it – a mental association evoked by the name of Mr. Porterfield. Surely I had a personal impression, over-smeared and confused, of the gentleman who was waiting at Liverpool, or who presently would be, for Mrs. Nettlepoint's protegee. I had met him, known him, some time, somewhere, somehow, on the other side. Wasn't he studying something, very hard, somewhere – probably in Paris – ten years before, and didn't he make extraordinarily neat drawings, linear and architectural? Didn't he go to a table d'hote, at two francs twenty-five, in the Rue Bonaparte, which I then frequented, and didn't he wear spectacles and a Scotch plaid arranged in a manner which seemed to say "I've trustworthy information that that's the way they do it in the Highlands"? Wasn't he exemplary to positive irritation, and very poor, poor to positive oppression, so that I supposed he had no overcoat and his tartan would be what he slept under at night? Wasn't he working very hard still, and wouldn't he be, in the natural course, not yet satisfied that he had found his feet or knew enough to launch out? He would be a man of long preparations – Miss Mavis's white face seemed to speak to one of that. It struck me that if I had been in love with her I shouldn't have needed to lay such a train for the closer approach. Architecture was his line and he was a pupil of the

Ecole des Beaux Arts. This reminiscence grew so much more vivid with me that at the end of ten minutes I had an odd sense of knowing – by implication – a good deal about the young lady.

Even after it was settled that Mrs. Nettlepoint would do everything possible for her the other visitor sat sipping our iced liquid and telling how "low" Mr. Mavis had been. At this period the girl's silence struck me as still more conscious, partly perhaps because she deprecated her mother's free flow – she was enough of an "improvement" to measure that – and partly because she was too distressed by the idea of leaving her infirm, her perhaps dying father. It wasn't indistinguishable that they were poor and that she would take out a very small purse for her trousseau. For Mr. Porterfield to make up the sum his own case would have had moreover greatly to change. If he had enriched himself by the successful practice of his profession I had encountered no edifice he had reared – his reputation hadn't come to my ears.

Mrs. Nettlepoint notified her new friends that she was a very inactive person at sea: she was prepared to suffer to the full with Miss Mavis, but not prepared to pace the deck with her, to struggle with her, to accompany her to meals. To this the girl replied that she would trouble her little, she was sure: she was convinced she should prove a wretched sailor and spend the voyage on her back. Her mother scoffed at this picture, prophesying perfect weather and a lovely time, and I interposed to the effect that if I might be trusted, as a tame bachelor fairly sea-seasoned, I should be delighted to give the new member of our party an arm or any other countenance whenever she should require it. Both the ladies thanked me for this – taking my professions with no sort of abatement – and the elder one declared that we were evidently going to be such a sociable group that it was too bad to have to stay at home. She asked Mrs. Nettlepoint if there were any one else in our party, and when our hostess mentioned her son – there was a chance of his embarking but (wasn't it absurd?) he hadn't decided yet – she returned with extraordinary candour: "Oh dear, I do hope he'll go: that would be so lovely for Grace."

Somehow the words made me think of poor Mr. Porterfield's tartan, especially as Jasper Nettlepoint strolled in again at that moment. His mother at once challenged him: it was ten o'clock; had he by chance made up his great mind? Apparently he failed to hear her, being in the first place surprised at the strange ladies and then struck with the fact that one of them wasn't strange. The young man, after a slight hesitation, greeted Miss Mavis with a handshake and a "Oh good-evening, how do you do?" He didn't utter her name – which I could see he must have forgotten; but she immediately pronounced his, availing herself of the American girl's discretion to "present" him to her mother.

"Well, you might have told me you knew him all this time!" that lady jovially cried. Then she had an equal confidence for Mrs. Nettlepoint. "It would have saved me a worry – an acquaintance already begun."

"Ah my son's acquaintances!" our hostess murmured.

"Yes, and my daughter's too!" Mrs. Mavis gaily echoed. "Mrs. Allen didn't tell us YOU were going," she continued to the young man.

"She'd have been clever if she had been able to!" Mrs. Nettlepoint sighed.

"Dear mother, I have my telegram," Jasper remarked, looking at Grace Mavis.

"I know you very little," the girl said, returning his observation.

"I've danced with you at some ball – for some sufferers by something or other."

"I think it was an inundation or a big fire," she a little languidly smiled. "But it was a long time ago – and I haven't seen you since."

"I've been in far countries – to my loss. I should have said it was a big fire."

"It was at the Horticultural Hall. I didn't remember your name," said Grace Mavis.

"That's very unkind of you, when I recall vividly that you had a pink dress."

"Oh I remember that dress – your strawberry tarletan: you looked lovely in it!" Mrs. Mavis broke out. "You must get another just like it – on the other side."

"Yes, your daughter looked charming in it," said Jasper Nettlepoint. Then he added to the girl: "Yet you mentioned my name to your mother."

"It came back to me – seeing you here. I had no idea this was your home."

"Well, I confess it isn't, much. Oh there are some drinks!" – he approached the tray and its glasses.

"Indeed there are and quite delicious" – Mrs. Mavis largely wiped her mouth.

"Won't you have another then? – a pink one, like your daughter's gown."

"With pleasure, sir. Oh do see them over," Mrs. Mavis continued, accepting from the young man's hand a third tumbler.

"My mother and that gentleman? Surely they can take care of themselves," he freely pleaded.

"Then my daughter – she has a claim as an old friend."

But his mother had by this time interposed. "Jasper, what does your telegram say?"

He paid her no heed: he stood there with his glass in his hand, looking from Mrs. Mavis to Miss Grace.

"Ah leave her to me, madam; I'm quite competent," I said to Mrs. Mavis.

Then the young man gave me his attention. The next minute he asked of the girl: "Do you mean you're going to Europe?"

"Yes, tomorrow. In the same ship as your mother."

"That's what we've come here for, to see all about it," said Mrs. Mavis.

"My son, take pity on me and tell me what light your telegram throws," Mrs. Nettlepoint went on.

"I will, dearest, when I've quenched my thirst." And he slowly drained his glass.

"Well, I declare you're worse than Gracie," Mrs. Mavis commented. "She was first one thing and then the other – but only about up to three o'clock yesterday."

"Excuse me – won't you take something?" Jasper inquired of Gracie; who however still declined, as if to make up for her mother's copious consommation. I found myself quite aware that the two ladies would do well to take leave, the question of Mrs. Nettlepoint's good will being so satisfactorily settled and the meeting of the morrow at the ship so near at hand and I went so far as to judge that their protracted stay, with their hostess visibly in a fidget, gave the last proof of their want of breeding. Miss Grace after all then was not such an improvement on her mother, for she easily might have taken the initiative of departure, in spite of Mrs. Mavis's evident "game" of making her own absorption of refreshment last as long as possible. I watched the girl with increasing interest; I couldn't help asking myself a question or two about her and even perceiving already (in a dim and general way) that rather marked embarrassment, or at least anxiety attended her. Wasn't it complicating that she should have needed, by remaining long enough, to assuage a certain suspense, to learn whether or no Jasper were going to sail? Hadn't something particular passed between them on the occasion or at the period to which we had caught their allusion, and didn't she really not know her mother was bringing her to HIS mother's, though she apparently had thought it well not to betray knowledge? Such things were symptomatic – though indeed one scarce knew of what – on the part of a young lady betrothed to that curious cross-barred phantom of a Mr. Porterfield. But I am bound to add that she gave me no further warrant for wonder than was conveyed in her all tacitly and covertly encouraging her mother to linger. Somehow I had a sense that SHE was conscious of the indecency of this. I got up myself to go, but Mrs. Nettlepoint detained me after seeing that my movement wouldn't be taken as a hint, and I felt she wished me not to leave my fellow visitors on her hands. Jasper complained of the closeness of the room, said that it was not a night to sit in a room – one ought to be out in the air, under the sky. He denounced the windows that overlooked the water for not opening upon a balcony or a terrace, until his mother, whom he hadn't yet satisfied about his telegram, reminded him that there was a beautiful balcony in front, with room for a dozen people. She assured him we would go and sit there if it would please him.

"It will be nice and cool tomorrow, when we steam into the great ocean," said Miss Mavis, expressing with more vivacity than she had yet thrown into any of her utterances my own thought of half an hour before. Mrs. Nettlepoint replied that it would probably be freezing cold, and her son murmured that he would go and try the drawing-room balcony and report upon it. Just as he was turning away he said, smiling, to Miss Mavis: "Won't you come with me and see if it's pleasant?"

"Oh well, we had better not stay all night!" her mother exclaimed, but still without moving. The girl moved, after a moment's hesitation; – she rose and accompanied Jasper to the other room. I saw how her slim tallness showed to advantage as she walked, and that she looked well as she passed, with her head thrown back, into the darkness of the other part of the house. There was something rather marked, rather surprising – I scarcely knew why, for the act in itself was simple enough – in her acceptance of such a plea, and perhaps it was our sense of this that held the rest of us somewhat stiffly silent as she remained away. I was waiting for Mrs. Mavis to go, so that I myself might go; and Mrs. Nettlepoint was waiting for her to go so that I mightn't. This doubtless made the young lady's absence appear to us longer than it really was – it was probably very brief. Her mother more-over, I think, had now a vague lapse from ease. Jasper Nettlepoint presently returned to the back drawing-room to serve his companion with our lucent syrup, and he took occasion to remark that it was lovely on the balcony: one really got some air, the breeze being from that quarter. I remembered, as he went away with his tinkling tumbler, that from MY hand, a few minutes before, Miss Mavis had not been willing to accept this innocent offering. A little later Mrs. Nettlepoint said: "Well, if it's so pleasant there we had better go ourselves." So we passed to the front and in the other room met the two young people coming in from the balcony. I was to wonder, in the light of later things, exactly how long they had occupied together a couple of the set of cane chairs garnishing the place in summer. If it had been but five minutes that only made subsequent events more curious. "We must go, mother," Miss Mavis immediately said; and a moment after, with a little renewal of chatter as to our general meeting on the ship, the visitors had taken leave. Jasper went down with them to the door and as soon as they had got off Mrs. Nettlepoint quite richly exhaled her impression. "Ah but'll she be a bore – she'll be a bore of bores!"

"Not through talking too much, surely."

"An affectation of silence is as bad. I hate that particular pose; it's coming up very much now; an imitation of the English, like everything else. A girl who tries to be statuesque at sea – that will act on one's nerves!"

"I don't know what she tries to be, but she succeeds in being very handsome."

"So much the better for you. I'll leave her to you, for I shall be shut up. I like her being placed under my 'care'!" my friend cried.

"She'll be under Jasper's," I remarked.

"Ah he won't go," she wailed – "I want it too much!"

"But I didn't see it that way. I have an idea he'll go."

"Why didn't he tell me so then – when he came in?"

"He was diverted by that young woman – a beautiful unexpected girl sitting there."

"Diverted from his mother and her fond hope? – his mother trembling for his decision?"

"Well" – I pieced it together – "she's an old friend, older than we know. It was a meeting after a long separation."

"Yes, such a lot of them as he does know!" Mrs. Nettlepoint sighed.

"Such a lot of them?"

"He has so many female friends – in the most varied circles."

"Well, we can close round her then," I returned; "for I on my side know, or used to know, her young man."

"Her intended?" – she had a light of relief for this.

"The very one she's going out to. He can't, by the way," it occurred to me, "be very young now."

"How odd it sounds – her muddling after him!" said Mrs. Nettlepoint.

I was going to reply that it wasn't odd if you knew Mr. Porterfield, but I reflected that that perhaps only made it odder. I told my companion briefly who he was – that I had met him in the old Paris days, when

I believed for a fleeting hour that I could learn to paint, when I lived with the jeunesse des ecoles; and her comment on this was simply: "Well, he had better have come out for her!"

"Perhaps so. She looked to me as she sat there as if, she might change her mind at the last moment."

"About her marriage?"

"About sailing. But she won't change now."

Jasper came back, and his mother instantly challenged him. "Well, ARE you going?"

"Yes, I shall go" – he was finally at peace about it. "I've got my telegram."

"Oh your telegram!" – I ventured a little to jeer.

"That charming girl's your telegram."

He gave me a look, but in the dusk I couldn't make out very well what it conveyed. Then he bent over his mother, kissing her. "My news isn't particularly satisfactory. I'm going for YOU."

"Oh you humbug!" she replied. But she was of course delighted.

CHAPTER II

People usually spend the first hours of a voyage in squeezing themselves into their cabins, taking their little precautions, either so excessive or so inadequate, wondering how they can pass so many days in such a hole and asking idiotic questions of the stewards, who appear in comparison rare men of the world. My own initiations were rapid, as became an old sailor, and so, it seemed, were Miss Mavis's, for when I mounted to the deck at the end of half an hour I found her there alone, in the stern of the ship, her eyes on the dwindling continent. It dwindled very fast for so big a place. I accosted her, having had no conversation with her amid the crowd of leave-takers and the muddle of farewells before we put off; we talked a little about the boat, our fellow-passengers and our prospects, and then I said: "I think you mentioned last night a name I know – that of Mr. Porterfield."

"Oh no I didn't!" she answered very straight while she smiled at me through her closely-drawn veil.

"Then it was your mother."

"Very likely it was my mother." And she continued to smile as if I ought to have known the difference.

"I venture to allude to him because I've an idea I used to know him," I went on.

"Oh I see." And beyond this remark she appeared to take no interest; she left it to me to make any connexion.

"That is if it's the same one." It struck me as feeble to say nothing more; so I added "My Mr. Porterfield was called David."

"Well, so is ours." "Ours" affected me as clever.

"I suppose I shall see him again if he's to meet you at Liverpool," I continued.

"Well, it will be bad if he doesn't."

It was too soon for me to have the idea that it would be bad if he did: that only came later. So I remarked that, not having seen him for so many years, it was very possible I shouldn't know him.

"Well, I've not seen him for a considerable time, but I expect I shall know him all the same."

"Oh with you it's different," I returned with harmlessly bright significance. "Hasn't he been back since those days?"

"I don't know," she sturdily professed, "what days you mean."

"When I knew him in Paris – ages ago. He was a pupil of the Ecole des Beaux Arts. He was studying architecture."

"Well, he's studying it still," said Grace Mavis.

"Hasn't he learned it yet?"

"I don't know what he has learned. I shall see." Then she added for the benefit of my perhaps undue levity: "Architecture's very difficult and he's tremendously thorough."

"Oh yes, I remember that. He was an admirable worker. But he must have become quite a foreigner if it's so many years since he has been at home."

She seemed to regard this proposition at first as complicated; but she did what she could for me. "Oh he's not changeable. If he were changeable–"

Then, however, she paused. I daresay she had been going to observe that if he were changeable he would long ago have given her up. After an instant she went on: "He wouldn't have stuck so to his profession. You can't make much by it."

I sought to attenuate her rather odd maidenly grimness. "It depends on what you call much."

"It doesn't make you rich."

"Oh of course you've got to practise it – and to practise it long."

"Yes – so Mr. Porterfield says."

Something in the way she uttered these words made me laugh – they were so calm an implication that the gentleman in question didn't live up to his principles. But I checked myself, asking her if she expected to remain in Europe long – to what one might call settle.

"Well, it will be a good while if it takes me as long to come back as it has taken me to go out."

"And I think your mother said last night that it was your first visit."

Miss Mavis, in her deliberate way, met my eyes. "Didn't mother talk!"

"It was all very interesting."

She continued to look at me. "You don't think that," she then simply stated.

"What have I to gain then by saying it?"

"Oh men have always something to gain."

"You make me in that case feel a terrible failure! I hope at any rate that it gives you pleasure," I went on, "the idea of seeing foreign lands."

"Mercy – I should think so!"

This was almost genial, and it cheered me proportionately. "It's a pity our ship's not one of the fast ones, if you're impatient."

She was silent a little after which she brought out: "Oh I guess it'll be fast enough!"

That evening I went in to see Mrs. Nettlepoint and sat on her sea-trunk, which was pulled out from under the berth to accommodate me. It was nine o'clock but not quite dark, as our northward course had already taken us into the latitude of the longer days. She had made her nest admirably and now rested from her labours; she lay upon her sofa in a dressing-gown and a cap that became her. It was her regular practice to spend the voyage in her cabin, which smelt positively good – such was the refinement of her art; and she had a secret peculiar to herself for keeping her port open without shipping seas. She hated what she called the mess of the ship and the idea, if she should go above, of meeting stewards with plates of supererogatory food. She professed to be content with her situation – we promised to lend each other books and I assured her familiarly that I should be in and out of her room a dozen times a day – pitying me for having to mingle in society. She judged this a limited privilege, for on the deck before we left the wharf she had taken a view of our fellow-passengers.

"Oh I'm an inveterate, almost a professional observer," I replied, "and with that vice I'm as well occupied as an old woman in the sun with her knitting. It makes me, in any situation, just inordinately and submissively SEE things. I shall see them even here and shall come down very often and tell you about them. You're not interested today, but you will be tomorrow, for a ship's a great school of gossip. You won't believe the number of researches and problems you'll be engaged in by the middle of the voyage."

"I? Never in the world! – lying here with my nose in a book and not caring a straw."

"You'll participate at second hand. You'll see through my eyes, hang upon my lips, take sides, feel passions, all sorts of sympathies and indignations. I've an idea," I further developed, "that your young lady's the person on board who will interest me most."

"'Mine' indeed! She hasn't been near me since we left the dock."

"There you are – you do feel she owes you something. Well," I added, "she's very curious."

"You've such cold-blooded terms!" Mrs. Nettlepoint wailed. "Elle ne sait pas se conduire; she ought to have come to ask about me."

"Yes, since you're under her care," I laughed. "As for her not knowing how to behave – well, that's exactly what we shall see."

"You will, but not I! I wash my hands of her."

"Don't say that – don't say that."

Mrs. Nettlepoint looked at me a moment. "Why do you speak so solemnly?"

In return I considered her. "I'll tell you before we land. And have you seen much of your son?"

"Oh yes, he has come in several times. He seems very much pleased. He has got a cabin to himself."

"That's great luck," I said, "but I've an idea he's always in luck. I was sure I should have to offer him the second berth in my room."

"And you wouldn't have enjoyed that, because you don't like him," she took upon herself to say.

"What put that into your head?"

"It isn't in my head – it's in my heart, my coeur de mere. We guess those things. You think he's selfish. I could see it last night."

"Dear lady," I contrived promptly enough to reply, "I've no general ideas about him at all. He's just one of the phenomena I am going to observe. He seems to me a very fine young man. However," I added, "since you've mentioned last night I'll admit that I thought he rather tantalised you. He played with your suspense."

"Why he came at the last just to please me," said Mrs. Nettlepoint.

I was silent a little. "Are you sure it was for your sake?"

"Ah, perhaps it was for yours!"

I bore up, however, against this thrust, characteristic of perfidious woman when you presume to side with her against a fond tormentor. "When he went out on the balcony with that girl," I found assurance to suggest, "perhaps she asked him to come for HERS."

"Perhaps she did. But why should he do everything she asks him – such as she is?"

"I don't know yet, but perhaps I shall know later. Not that he'll tell me – for he'll never tell me anything: he's not," I consistently opined, "one of those who tell."

"If she didn't ask him, what you say is a great wrong to her," said Mrs. Nettlepoint.

"Yes, if she didn't. But you say that to protect Jasper – not to protect her," I smiled.

"You ARE cold-blooded – it's uncanny!" my friend exclaimed.

"Ah this is nothing yet! Wait a while – you'll see. At sea in general I'm awful – I exceed the limits. If I've outraged her in thought I'll jump overboard. There are ways of asking – a man doesn't need to tell a woman that – without the crude words."

"I don't know what you imagine between them," said Mrs. Nettlepoint.

"Well, nothing," I allowed, "but what was visible on the surface. It transpired, as the newspapers say, that they were old friends."

"He met her at some promiscuous party – I asked him about it afterwards. She's not a person" – my hostess was confident – "whom he could ever think of seriously."

"That's exactly what I believe."

"You don't observe – you know – you imagine," Mrs. Nettlepoint continued to argue. "How do you reconcile her laying a trap for Jasper with her going out to Liverpool on an errand of love?"

Oh I wasn't to be caught that way! "I don't for an instant suppose she laid a trap; I believe she acted on the impulse of the moment. She's going out to Liverpool on an errand of marriage; that's not necessarily the same thing as an errand of love, especially for one who happens to have had a personal impression of the gentleman she's engaged to."

"Well, there are certain decencies which in such a situation the most abandoned of her sex would still observe. You apparently judge her capable – on no evidence – of violating them."

"Ah you don't understand the shades of things," I returned. "Decencies and violations, dear lady – there's no need for such heavy artillery! I can perfectly imagine that without the least immodesty she should have said to Jasper on the balcony, in fact if not in words: 'I'm in dreadful spirits, but if you come I shall feel better, and that will be pleasant for you too.–"

"And why is she in dreadful spirits?"

"She isn't!" I replied, laughing.

My poor friend wondered. "What then is she doing?"

"She's walking with your son."

Mrs. Nettlepoint for a moment said nothing; then she treated me to another inconsequence. "Ah she's horrid!"

"No, she's charming!" I protested.

"You mean she's 'curious'?"

"Well, for me it's the same thing!"

This led my friend of course to declare once more that I was cold-blooded. On the afternoon of the morrow we had another talk, and she told me that in the morning Miss Mavis had paid her a long visit. She knew nothing, poor creature, about anything, but her intentions were good and she was evidently in her own eyes conscientious and decorous. And Mrs. Nettlepoint concluded these remarks with the sigh "Unfortunate person!"

"You think she's a good deal to be pitied then?"

"Well, her story sounds dreary – she told me a good deal of it. She fell to talking little by little and went from one thing to another. She's in that situation when a girl MUST open herself – to some woman."

"Hasn't she got Jasper?" I asked.

"He isn't a woman. You strike me as jealous of him," my companion added.

"I daresay HE thinks so – or will before the end. Ah no – ah no!" And I asked Mrs. Nettlepoint if our young lady struck her as, very grossly, a flirt. She gave me no answer, but went on to remark that she found it odd and interesting to see the way a girl like Grace Mavis resembled the girls of the kind she herself knew better, the girls of "society," at the same time that she differed from them; and the way the differences and resemblances were so mixed up that on certain questions you couldn't tell where you'd find her. You'd think she'd feel as you did because you had found her feeling so, and then suddenly, in regard to some other matter – which was yet quite the same – she'd be utterly wanting. Mrs. Nettlepoint proceeded to observe – to such idle speculations does the vacancy of sea-hours give encouragement – that she wondered whether it were better to be an ordinary girl very well brought up or an extraordinary girl not brought up at all.

"Oh I go in for the extraordinary girl under all circumstances."

"It's true that if you're VERY well brought up you're not, you can't be, ordinary," said Mrs. Nettle-point, smelling her strong salts. "You're a lady, at any rate."

"And Miss Mavis is fifty miles out – is that what you mean?"

"Well – you've seen her mother."

"Yes, but I think your contention would be that among such people the mother doesn't count."

"Precisely, and that's bad."

"I see what you mean. But isn't it rather hard? If your mother doesn't know anything it's better you should be independent of her, and yet if you are that constitutes a bad note." I added that Mrs. Mavis had appeared to count sufficiently two nights before. She had said and done everything she wanted, while the girl sat silent and respectful. Grace's attitude, so far as her parent was concerned, had been eminently decent.

"Yes, but she 'squirmed' for her," said Mrs. Nettlepoint.

"Ah if you know it I may confess she has told me as much."

My friend stared. "Told YOU? There's one of the things they do!"

"Well, it was only a word. Won't you let me know whether you do think her a flirt?"

"Try her yourself – that's better than asking another woman; especially as you pretend to study folk."

"Oh your judgement wouldn't probably at all determine mine. It's as bearing on YOU I ask it." Which, however, demanded explanation, so that I was duly frank; confessing myself curious as to how far maternal immorality would go.

It made her at first but repeat my words. "Maternal immorality?"

"You desire your son to have every possible distraction on his voyage, and if you can make up your mind in the sense I refer to that will make it all right. He'll have no responsibility."

"Heavens, how you analyse!" she cried. "I haven't in the least your passion for making up my mind."

"Then if you chance it," I returned, "you'll be more immoral still."

"Your reasoning's strange," said Mrs. Nettlepoint; "when it was you who tried to put into my head yesterday that she had asked him to come."

"Yes, but in good faith."

"What do you mean, in such a case, by that?"

"Why, as girls of that sort do. Their allowance and measure in such matters," I expounded, "is much larger than that of young persons who have been, as you say, VERY well brought up; and yet I'm not sure that on the whole I don't think them thereby the more innocent. Miss Mavis is engaged, and she's to be married next week, but it's an old old story, and there's no more romance in it than if she were going to be photographed. So her usual life proceeds, and her usual life consists – and that of ces demoiselles in general – in having plenty of gentlemen's society. Having it I mean without having any harm from it."

Mrs. Nettlepoint had given me due attention. "Well, if there's no harm from it what are you talking about and why am I immoral?"

I hesitated, laughing. "I retract – you're sane and clear. I'm sure she thinks there won't be any harm," I added. "That's the great point."

"The great point?"

"To be settled, I mean."

"Mercy, we're not trying them!" cried my friend. "How can WE settle it?"

"I mean of course in our minds. There will be nothing more interesting these next ten days for our minds to exercise themselves upon."

"Then they'll get terribly tired of it," said Mrs. Nettlepoint.

"No, no – because the interest will increase and the plot will thicken. It simply can't NOT," I insisted. She looked at me as if she thought me more than Mephistophelean, and I went back to something she had lately mentioned. "So she told you everything in her life was dreary?"

"Not everything, but most things. And she didn't tell me so much as I guessed it. She'll tell me more the next time. She'll behave properly now about coming in to see me; I told her she ought to."

"I'm glad of that," I said. "Keep her with you as much as possible."

"I don't follow you closely," Mrs. Nettlepoint replied, "but so far as I do I don't think your remarks in the best taste."

"Well, I'm too excited, I lose my head in these sports," I had to recognise "cold-blooded as you think me. Doesn't she like Mr. Porterfield?"

"Yes, that's the worst of it."

I kept making her stare. "The worst of it?"

"He's so good – there's no fault to be found with him. Otherwise she'd have thrown it all up. It has dragged on since she was eighteen: she became engaged to him before he went abroad to study. It was one of those very young and perfectly needless blunders that parents in America might make so much less possible than they do. The thing is to insist on one's daughter waiting, on the engagement's being long; and then, after you've got that started, to take it on every occasion as little seriously as possible – to make it die out. You can easily tire it to death," Mrs. Nettlepoint competently stated. "However," she concluded, "Mr. Porterfield has taken this one seriously for some years. He has done his part to keep it alive. She says he adores her."

"His part? Surely his part would have been to marry her by this time."

"He has really no money." My friend was even more confidently able to report it than I had been.

"He ought to have got some, in seven years," I audibly reflected.

"So I think she thinks. There are some sorts of helplessness that are contemptible. However, a small difference has taken place. That's why he won't wait any longer. His mother has come out, she has something – a little – and she's able to assist him. She'll live with them and bear some of the expenses, and after her death the son will have what there is."

"How old is she?" I cynically asked.

"I haven't the least idea. But it doesn't, on his part, sound very heroic – or very inspiring for our friend here. He hasn't been to America since he first went out."

"That's an odd way of adoring her," I observed.

"I made that objection mentally, but I didn't express it to her. She met it indeed a little by telling me that he had had other chances to marry."

"That surprises me," I remarked. "But did she say," I asked, "that SHE had had?"

"No, and that's one of the things I thought nice in her; for she must have had. She didn't try to make out that he had spoiled her life. She has three other sisters and there's very little money at home. She has tried to make money; she has written little things and painted little things – and dreadful little things they must have been; too bad to think of. Her father has had a long illness and has lost his place – he was in receipt of a salary in connexion with some waterworks – and one of her sisters has lately become a widow, with children and without means. And so as in fact she never has married any one else, whatever opportunities she may have encountered, she appears to have just made up her mind to go out to Mr. Porterfield as the least of her evils. But it isn't very amusing."

"Well," I judged after all, "that only makes her doing it the more honourable. She'll go through with it, whatever it costs, rather than disappoint him after he has waited so long. It's true," I continued, "that when a woman acts from a sense of honour–!"

"Well, when she does?" said Mrs. Nettlepoint, for I hung back perceptibly.

"It's often so extravagant and unnatural a proceeding as to entail heavy costs on some one."

"You're very impertinent. We all have to pay for each other all the while and for each other's virtues as well as vices."

"That's precisely why I shall be sorry for Mr. Porterfield when she steps off the ship with her little bill. I mean with her teeth clenched."

"Her teeth are not in the least clenched. She's quite at her ease now" – Mrs. Nettlepoint could answer for that.

"Well, we must try and keep her so," I said.

"You must take care that Jasper neglects nothing." I scarce know what reflexions this innocent pleasantry of mine provoked on the good lady's part; the upshot of them at all events was to make her say: "Well, I never asked her to come; I'm very glad of that. It's all their own doing."

"'Their' own – you mean Jasper's and hers?"

"No indeed. I mean her mother's and Mrs. Allen's; the girl's too of course. They put themselves on us by main force."

"Oh yes, I can testify to that. Therefore I'm glad too. We should have missed it, I think."

"How seriously you take it!" Mrs. Nettlepoint amusedly cried.

"Ah wait a few days!" – and I got up to leave her.

CHAPTER III

The Patagonia was slow, but spacious and comfortable, and there was a motherly decency in her long nursing rock and her rustling old-fashioned gait, the multitudinous swish, in her wake, as of a thousand proper petticoats. It was as if she wished not to present herself in port with the splashed eagerness of a young creature. We weren't numerous enough quite to elbow each other and yet weren't too few to support – with that familiarity and relief which figures and objects acquire on the great bare field of the ocean and under the great bright glass of the sky. I had never liked the sea so much before, indeed I had never liked it at all; but now I had a revelation of how in a midsummer mood it could please. It was darkly and magnificently blue and imperturbably quiet – save for the great regular swell of its heartbeats, the pulse of its life; and there grew to be something so agreeable in the sense of floating there in infinite isolation and leisure that it was a positive godsend the Patagonia was no racer. One had never thought of the sea as the great place of safety, but now it came over one that there's no place so safe from the land. When it doesn't confer trouble it takes trouble away – takes away letters and telegrams and newspapers and visits and duties and efforts, all the complications, all the superfluities and superstitions that we have stuffed into our terrene life. The simple absence of the post, when the particular conditions enable you to enjoy the great fact by which it's produced, becomes in itself a positive bliss, and the clean boards of the deck turn to the stage of a play that amuses, the personal drama of the voyage, the movement and interaction, in the strong sea-light, of figures that end by representing something – something moreover of which the interest is never, even in its keenness, too great to suffer you to slumber. I at any rate dozed to excess, stretched on my rug with a French novel, and when I opened my eyes I generally saw Jasper Nettlepoint pass with the young woman confided to his mother's care on his arm. Somehow at these moments, between sleeping and waking, I inconsequently felt that my French novel had set them in motion. Perhaps this was because I had fallen into the trick, at the start, of regarding Grace Mavis almost as a married woman, which, as every one knows, is the necessary status of the heroine of such a work. Every revolution of our engine at any rate would contribute to the effect of making her one.

In the saloon, at meals, my neighbour on the right was a certain little Mrs. Peck, a very short and very round person whose head was enveloped in a "cloud" (a cloud of dirty white wool) and who promptly let me know that she was going to Europe for the education of her children. I had already perceived – an hour after we left the dock – that some energetic measure was required in their interest, but as we were not in

Europe yet the redemption of the four little Pecks was stayed. Enjoying untrammelled leisure they swarmed about the ship as if they had been pirates boarding her, and their mother was as powerless to check their licence as if she had been gagged and stowed away in the hold. They were especially to be trusted to dive between the legs of the stewards when these attendants arrived with bowls of soup for the languid ladies. Their mother was too busy counting over to her fellow-passengers all the years Miss Mavis had been engaged. In the blank of our common detachment things that were nobody's business very soon became everybody's, and this was just one of those facts that are propagated with mysterious and ridiculous speed. The whisper that carries them is very small, in the great scale of things, of air and space and progress, but it's also very safe, for there's no compression, no sounding-board, to make speakers responsible. And then repetition at sea is somehow not repetition; monotony is in the air, the mind is flat and everything recurs – the bells, the meals, the stewards' faces, the romp of children, the walk, the clothes, the very shoes and buttons of passengers taking their exercise. These things finally grow at once so circumstantial and so arid that, in comparison, lights on the personal history of one's companions become a substitute for the friendly flicker of the lost fireside.

Jasper Nettlepoint sat on my left hand when he was not upstairs seeing that Miss Mavis had her repast comfortably on deck. His mother's place would have been next mine had she shown herself, and then that of the young lady under her care. These companions, in other words, would have been between us, Jasper marking the limit of the party in that quarter. Miss Mavis was present at luncheon the first day, but dinner passed without her coming in, and when it was half over Jasper remarked that he would go up and look after her.

"Isn't that young lady coming – the one who was here to lunch?" Mrs. Peck asked of me as he left the saloon.

"Apparently not. My friend tells me she doesn't like the saloon."

"You don't mean to say she's sick, do you?"

"Oh no, not in this weather. But she likes to be above."

"And is that gentleman gone up to her?"

"Yes, she's under his mother's care."

"And is his mother up there, too?" asked Mrs. Peck, whose processes were homely and direct.

"No, she remains in her cabin. People have different tastes. Perhaps that's one reason why Miss Mavis doesn't come to table," I added – "her chaperon not being able to accompany her."

"Her chaperon?" my fellow passenger echoed.

"Mrs. Nettlepoint the lady under whose protection she happens to be."

"Protection?" Mrs. Peck stared at me a moment, moving some valued morsel in her mouth; then she exclaimed familiarly "Pshaw!" I was struck with this and was on the point of asking her what she meant by it when she continued: "Ain't we going to see Mrs. Nettlepoint?"

"I'm afraid not. She vows she won't stir from her sofa."

"Pshaw!" said Mrs. Peck again. "That's quite a disappointment."

"Do you know her then?"

"No, but I know all about her." Then my companion added: "You don't mean to say she's any real relation?"

"Do you mean to me?"

"No, to Grace Mavis."

"None at all. They're very new friends, as I happen to know. Then you're acquainted with our young lady?" I hadn't noticed the passage of any recognition between them at luncheon.

"Is she your young lady too?" asked Mrs. Peck with high significance.

"Ah when people are in the same boat – literally – they belong a little to each other."

"That's so," said Mrs. Peck. "I don't know Miss Mavis, but I know all about her – I live opposite to her on Merrimac Avenue. I don't know whether you know that part."

"Oh yes – it's very beautiful."

The consequence of this remark was another "Pshaw!" But Mrs. Peck went on: "When you've lived opposite to people like that for a long time you feel as if you had some rights in them – tit for tat! But she didn't take it up today; she didn't speak to me. She knows who I am as well as she knows her own mother."

"You had better speak to her first – she's constitutionally shy," I remarked.

"Shy? She's constitutionally tough! Why she's thirty years old," cried my neighbour. "I suppose you know where she's going."

"Oh yes – we all take an interest in that."

"That young man, I suppose, particularly." And then as I feigned a vagueness: "The handsome one who sits THERE. Didn't you tell me he's Mrs. Nettlepoint's son?"

"Oh yes – he acts as her deputy. No doubt he does all he can to carry out her function."

Mrs. Peck briefly brooded. I had spoken jocosely, but she took it with a serious face. "Well, she might let him eat his dinner in peace!" she presently put forth.

"Oh he'll come back!" I said, glancing at his place. The repast continued and when it was finished I screwed my chair round to leave the table. Mrs. Peck performed the same movement and we quitted the saloon together. Outside of it was the usual vestibule, with several seats, from which you could descend to the lower cabins or mount to the promenade-deck. Mrs. Peck appeared to hesitate as to her course and then solved the problem by going neither way. She dropped on one of the benches and looked up at me.

"I thought you said he'd come back."

"Young Nettlepoint? Yes, I see he didn't. Miss Mavis then has given him half her dinner."

"It's very kind of her! She has been engaged half her life."

"Yes, but that will soon be over."

"So I suppose – as quick as ever we land. Every one knows it on Merrimac Avenue," Mrs. Peck pursued. "Every one there takes a great interest in it."

"Ah of course – a girl like that has many friends."

But my informant discriminated. "I mean even people who don't know her."

"I see," I went on: "she's so handsome that she attracts attention – people enter into her affairs."

Mrs. Peck spoke as from the commanding centre of these. "She USED to be pretty, but I can't say I think she's anything remarkable today. Anyhow, if she attracts attention she ought to be all the more careful what she does. You had better tell her that."

"Oh it's none of my business!" I easily made out, leaving the terrible little woman and going above. This profession, I grant, was not perfectly attuned to my real idea, or rather my real idea was not quite in harmony with my profession. The very first thing I did on reaching the deck was to notice that Miss Mavis was pacing it on Jasper Nettlepoint's arm and that whatever beauty she might have lost, according to Mrs. Peck's insinuation, she still kept enough to make one's eyes follow her. She had put on a crimson hood, which was very becoming to her and which she wore for the rest of the voyage. She walked very well, with long steps, and I remember that at this moment the sea had a gentle evening swell which made the great ship dip slowly, rhythmically, giving a movement that was graceful to graceful pedestrians and a more awkward one to the awkward. It was the loveliest hour of a fine day, the clear early evening, with the glow of the sunset in the air and a purple colour on the deep. It was always present to me that so the waters ploughed by the Homeric heroes must have looked. I became conscious on this particular occasion moreover that Grace Mavis would for the rest of the voyage be the most visible thing in one's range, the figure that would count most in the composition of groups. She couldn't help it, poor girl; nature had made her conspicuous – important, as the painters say. She paid for it by the corresponding exposure, the danger that people would, as I had said to Mrs. Peck, enter into her affairs.

Jasper Nettlepoint went down at certain times to see his mother, and I watched for one of these occasions – on the third day out – and took advantage of it to go and sit by Miss Mavis. She wore a light blue veil drawn tightly over her face, so that if the smile with which she greeted me rather lacked intensity I could account for it partly by that.

"Well, we're getting on – we're getting on," I said cheerfully, looking at the friendly twinkling sea.

"Are we going very fast?"

"Not fast, but steadily. Ohne Hast, ohne Rast – do you know German?"

"Well, I've studied it – some."

"It will be useful to you over there when you travel."

"Well yes, if we do. But I don't suppose we shall much. Mr. Nettlepoint says we ought," my young woman added in a moment.

"Ah of course HE thinks so. He has been all over the world."

"Yes, he has described some of the places. They must be wonderful. I didn't know I should like it so much."

"But it isn't 'Europe' yet!" I laughed.

Well, she didn't care if it wasn't. "I mean going on this way. I could go on for ever – for ever and ever."

"Ah you know it's not always like this," I hastened to mention.

"Well, it's better than Boston."

"It isn't so good as Paris," I still more portentously noted.

"Oh I know all about Paris. There's no freshness in that. I feel as if I had been there all the time."

"You mean you've heard so much of it?"

"Oh yes, nothing else for ten years."

I had come to talk with Miss Mavis because she was attractive, but I had been rather conscious of the absence of a good topic, not feeling at liberty to revert to Mr. Porterfield. She hadn't encouraged me, when I spoke to her as we were leaving Boston, to go on with the history of my acquaintance with this gentleman; and yet now, unexpectedly, she appeared to imply – it was doubtless one of the disparities mentioned by Mrs. Nettlepoint – that he might be glanced at without indelicacy.

"I see – you mean by letters," I remarked.

"We won't live in a good part. I know enough to know that," she went on.

"Well, it isn't as if there were any very bad ones," I answered reassuringly.

"Why Mr. Nettlepoint says it's regular mean."

"And to what does he apply that expression?"

She eyed me a moment as if I were elegant at her expense, but she answered my question. "Up there in the Batignolles. I seem to make out it's worse than Merrimac Avenue."

"Worse – in what way?"

"Why, even less where the nice people live."

"He oughtn't to say that," I returned. And I ventured to back it up. "Don't you call Mr. Porterfield a nice person?"

"Oh it doesn't make any difference." She watched me again a moment through her veil, the texture of which gave her look a suffused prettiness. "Do you know him very little?" she asked.

"Mr. Porterfield?"

"No, Mr. Nettlepoint."

"Ah very little. He's very considerably my junior, you see."

She had a fresh pause, as if almost again for my elegance; but she went on: "He's younger than me too." I don't know what effect of the comic there could have been in it, but the turn was unexpected and it made me laugh. Neither do I know whether Miss Mavis took offence at my sensibility on this head, though I remember thinking at the moment with compunction that it had brought a flush to her cheek. At all events she got up, gathering her shawl and her books into her arm. "I'm going down – I'm tired."

"Tired of me, I'm afraid."

"No, not yet."

"I'm like you," I confessed. "I should like it to go on and on."

She had begun to walk along the deck to the companionway and I went with her. "Well, I guess I wouldn't, after all!"

I had taken her shawl from her to carry it, but at the top of the steps that led down to the cabins I had to give it back. "Your mother would be glad if she could know," I observed as we parted.

But she was proof against my graces. "If she could know what?"

"How well you're getting on." I refused to be discouraged. "And that good Mrs. Allen."

"Oh mother, mother! She made me come, she pushed me off." And almost as if not to say more she went quickly below.

I paid Mrs. Nettlepoint a morning visit after luncheon and another in the evening, before she "turned in." That same day, in the evening, she said to me suddenly: "Do you know what I've done? I've asked Jasper."

"Asked him what?"

"Why, if SHE asked him, you understand."

I wondered. "DO I understand?"

"If you don't it's because you 'regular' won't, as she says. If that girl really asked him – on the balcony – to sail with us."

"My dear lady, do you suppose that if she did he'd tell you?"

She had to recognise my acuteness. "That's just what he says. But he says she didn't."

"And do you consider the statement valuable?" I asked, laughing out. "You had better ask your young friend herself."

Mrs. Nettlepoint stared. "I couldn't do that."

On which I was the more amused that I had to explain I was only amused. "What does it signify now?"

"I thought you thought everything signified. You were so full," she cried, "of signification!"

"Yes, but we're further out now, and somehow in mid-ocean everything becomes absolute."

"What else CAN he do with decency?" Mrs. Nettlepoint went on. "If, as my son, he were never to speak to her it would be very rude and you'd think that stranger still. Then YOU would do what he does, and where would be the difference?"

"How do you know what he does? I haven't mentioned him for twenty-four hours."

"Why, she told me herself. She came in this afternoon."

"What an odd thing to tell you!" I commented.

"Not as she says it. She says he's full of attention, perfectly devoted – looks after her all the time. She seems to want me to know it, so that I may approve him for it."

"That's charming; it shows her good conscience."

"Yes, or her great cleverness."

Something in the tone in which Mrs. Nettlepoint said this caused me to return in real surprise: "Why what do you suppose she has in her mind?"

"To get hold of him, to make him go so far he can't retreat. To marry him perhaps."

"To marry him? And what will she do with Mr. Porterfield?"

"She'll ask me just to make it all right to him – or perhaps you."

"Yes, as an old friend" – and for a moment I felt it awkwardly possible. But I put to her seriously: "DO you see Jasper caught like that?"

"Well, he's only a boy – he's younger at least than she."

"Precisely; she regards him as a child. She remarked to me herself today, that is, that he's so much younger."

Mrs. Nettlepoint took this in. "Does she talk of it with you? That shows she has a plan, that she has thought it over!"

I've sufficiently expressed – for the interest of my anecdote – that I found an oddity in one of our young companions, but I was far from judging her capable of laying a trap for the other. Moreover my reading of Jasper wasn't in the least that he was catchable – could be made to do a thing if he didn't want to do it. Of course it wasn't impossible that he might be inclined, that he might take it – or already have taken it – into his head to go further with his mother's charge; but to believe this I should require still more proof than his always being with her. He wanted at most to "take up with her" for the voyage. "If you've questioned him perhaps you've tried to make him feel responsible," I said to my fellow critic.

"A little, but it's very difficult. Interference makes him perverse. One has to go gently. Besides, it's too absurd – think of her age. If she can't take care of herself!" cried Mrs. Nettlepoint.

"Yes, let us keep thinking of her age, though it's not so prodigious. And if things get very bad you've one resource left," I added.

She wondered. "To lock her up in her cabin?"

"No – to come out of yours."

"Ah never, never! If it takes that to save her she must be lost. Besides, what good would it do? If I were to go above she could come below."

"Yes, but you could keep Jasper with you."

"COULD I?" Mrs. Nettlepoint demanded in the manner of a woman who knew her son.

In the saloon the next day, after dinner, over the red cloth of the tables, beneath the swinging lamps and the racks of tumblers, decanters and wineglasses, we sat down to whist, Mrs. Peck, to oblige, taking a hand in the game. She played very badly and talked too much, and when the rubber was over assuaged her discomfiture (though not mine – we had been partners) with a Welsh rabbit and a tumbler of something hot. We had done with the cards, but while she waited for this refreshment she sat with her elbows on the table shuffling a pack.

"She hasn't spoken to me yet – she won't do it," she remarked in a moment.

"Is it possible there's any one on the ship who hasn't spoken to you?"

"Not that girl – she knows too well!" Mrs. Peck looked round our little circle with a smile of intelligence – she had familiar communicative eyes. Several of our company had assembled, according to the wont, the last thing in the evening, of those who are cheerful at sea, for the consumption of grilled sardines and devilled bones.

"What then does she know?"

"Oh she knows I know."

"Well, we know what Mrs. Peck knows," one of the ladies of the group observed to me with an air of privilege.

"Well, you wouldn't know if I hadn't told you – from the way she acts," said our friend with a laugh of small charm.

"She's going out to a gentleman who lives over there – he's waiting there to marry her," the other lady went on, in the tone of authentic information. I remember that her name was Mrs. Gotch and that her mouth looked always as if she were whistling.

"Oh he knows – I've told him," said Mrs. Peck.

"Well, I presume every one knows," Mrs. Gotch contributed.

"Dear madam, is it every one's business?" I asked.

"Why, don't you think it's a peculiar way to act?" – and Mrs. Gotch was evidently surprised at my little protest.

"Why it's right there – straight in front of you, like a play at the theatre – as if you had paid to see it," said Mrs. Peck. "If you don't call it public!"

"Aren't you mixing things up? What do you call public?"

"Why the way they go on. They're up there now."

"They cuddle up there half the night," said Mrs. Gotch. "I don't know when they come down. Any hour they like. When all the lights are out they're up there still."

"Oh you can't tire them out. They don't want relief – like the ship's watch!" laughed one of the gentlemen.

"Well, if they enjoy each other's society what's the harm?" another asked. "They'd do just the same on land."

"They wouldn't do it on the public streets, I presume," said Mrs. Peck. "And they wouldn't do it if Mr. Porterfield was round!"

"Isn't that just where your confusion comes in?" I made answer. "It's public enough that Miss Mavis and Mr. Nettlepoint are always together, but it isn't in the least public that she's going to be married."

"Why how can you say – when the very sailors know it! The Captain knows it and all the officers know it. They see them there, especially at night, when they're sailing the ship."

"I thought there was some rule–!" submitted Mrs. Gotch.

"Well, there is – that you've got to behave yourself," Mrs. Peck explained. "So the Captain told me – he said they have some rule. He said they have to have, when people are too undignified."

"Is that the term he used?" I inquired.

"Well, he may have said when they attract too much attention."

I ventured to discriminate. "It's we who attract the attention – by talking about what doesn't concern us and about what we really don't know."

"She said the Captain said he'd tell on her as soon as ever we arrive," Mrs. Gotch none the less serenely pursued.

"SHE said-?" I repeated, bewildered.

"Well, he did say so, that he'd think it his duty to inform Mr. Porterfield when he comes on to meet her – if they keep it up in the same way," said Mrs. Peck.

"Oh they'll keep it up, don't you fear!" one of the gentlemen exclaimed.

"Dear madam, the Captain's having his joke on you," was, however, my own congruous reply.

"No, he ain't – he's right down scandalised. He says he regards us all as a real family and wants the family not to be downright coarse." I felt Mrs. Peck irritated by my controversial tone: she challenged me with considerable spirit. "How can you say I don't know it when all the street knows it and has known it for years – for years and years?" She spoke as if the girl had been engaged at least for twenty. "What's she going out for if not to marry him?"

"Perhaps she's going to see how he looks," suggested one of the gentlemen.

"He'd look queer – if he knew."

"Well, I guess he'll know," said Mrs. Gotch.

"She'd tell him herself – she wouldn't be afraid," the gentleman went on.

"Well she might as well kill him. He'll jump over-board," Mrs. Peck could foretell.

"Jump overboard?" cried Mrs. Gotch as if she hoped then that Mr. Porterfield would be told.

"He has just been waiting for this – for long, long years," said Mrs. Peck.

"Do you happen to know him?" I asked.

She replied at her convenience. "No, but I know a lady who does. Are you going up?"

I had risen from my place – I had not ordered supper. "I'm going to take a turn before going to bed."

"Well then you'll see!"

Outside the saloon I hesitated, for Mrs. Peck's admonition made me feel for a moment that if I went up I should have entered in a manner into her little conspiracy. But the night was so warm and splendid that I had been intending to smoke a cigar in the air before going below, and I didn't see why I should deprive myself of this pleasure in order to seem not to mind Mrs. Peck. I mounted accordingly and saw a few figures sitting or moving about in the darkness. The ocean looked black and small, as it is apt to do at night, and the long mass of the ship, with its vague dim wings, seemed to take up a great part of it. There were more stars than one saw on land and the heavens struck one more than ever as larger than the earth. Grace Mavis and her companion were not, so far as I perceived at first, among the few passengers who lingered late, and I was glad, because I hated to hear her talked about in the manner of the gossips I had left at supper. I wished there had been some way to prevent it, but I could think of none but to recommend her privately to reconsider her rule of discretion. That would be a very delicate business, and perhaps it would be better to begin with Jasper, though that would be delicate too. At any rate one might let him know, in a friendly spirit, to how much remark he exposed the young lady – leaving this revelation to work its way upon him. Unfortunately I couldn't altogether believe that the pair were unconscious of the observation and the opinion of the passengers. They weren't boy and girl; they had a certain social perspective in their eye. I was meanwhile at any rate in no possession of the details of that behaviour which had made them – according to the version of my good friends in the saloon – a scandal to the ship; for though I had taken due note of them, as will already have been gathered, I had taken really no such ferocious, or at least such competent, note as Mrs. Peck. Nevertheless the probability was that they knew what was thought of them – what naturally would be – and simply didn't care. That made our heroine out rather perverse and even rather shameless; and yet somehow if these were her leanings I didn't dislike her for them. I don't know what strange secret excuses I found for her. I presently indeed encountered, on the spot, a need for any I might have at call, since, just as I was on the point of going below again, after several restless turns and – within the limit where smoking was allowed – as many puffs at a cigar as I cared for, I became aware of a couple of figures settled together behind one of the lifeboats that rested on the deck. They were so placed as to be visible only to a person going close to the rail and peering a little sidewise. I don't think I peered, but as I stood a moment beside the rail my eye was attracted by a dusky object that protruded beyond the boat and that I saw at a second glance to be the tail of a lady's dress. I bent forward an instant, but even then I saw very little more; that scarcely mattered however, as I easily concluded that the persons tucked away in so snug a corner were Jasper Nettlepoint and Mr. Porterfield's intended. Tucked away was the odious right expression, and I deplored the fact so betrayed for the pitiful bad taste in it. I immediately turned away, and the next moment found myself face to face with our vessel's skipper. I had already had some conversation with him – he had been so good as to invite me, as he had invited Mrs. Nettlepoint and her son and the young lady travelling with them, and also Mrs. Peck, to sit at his table – and had observed with pleasure that his seamanship had the grace, not universal on the Atlantic liners, of a fine-weather manner.

"They don't waste much time – your friends in there," he said, nodding in the direction in which he had seen me looking.

"Ah well, they haven't much to lose."

"That's what I mean. I'm told SHE hasn't."

I wanted to say something exculpatory, but scarcely knew what note to strike. I could only look vaguely about me at the starry darkness and the sea that seemed to sleep. "Well, with these splendid nights and this perfect air people are beguiled into late hours."

"Yes, we want a bit of a blow," the Captain said.

I demurred. "How much of one?"

"Enough to clear the decks!"

He was after all rather dry and he went about his business. He had made me uneasy, and instead of going below I took a few turns more. The other walkers dropped off pair by pair – they were all men – till at last I was alone. Then after a little I quitted the field. Jasper and his companion were still behind their lifeboat. Personally I greatly preferred our actual conditions, but as I went down I found myself vaguely wishing, in the interest of I scarcely knew what, unless it had been a mere superstitious delicacy, that we might have half a gale.

Miss Mavis turned out, in sea-phrase, early; for the next morning I saw her come up only a short time after I had finished my breakfast, a ceremony over which I contrived not to dawdle. She was alone and Jasper Nettlepoint, by a rare accident, was not on deck to help her. I went to meet her – she was encumbered as usual with her shawl, her sun-umbrella and a book – and laid my hands on her chair, placing it near the stern of the ship, where she liked best to be. But I proposed to her to walk a little before she sat down, and she took my arm after I had put her accessories into the chair. The deck was clear at that hour and the morning light gay; one had an extravagant sense of good omens and propitious airs. I forget what we spoke of first, but it was because I felt these things pleasantly; and not to torment my companion nor to test her, that I couldn't help exclaiming cheerfully after a moment, as I have mentioned having done the first day: "Well, we're getting on, we're getting on!"

"Oh yes, I count every hour."

"The last days always go quicker," I said, "and the last hours–!"

"Well, the last hours?" she asked; for I had instinctively checked myself.

"Oh one's so glad then that it's almost the same as if one had arrived. Yet we ought to be grateful when the elements have been so kind to us," I added. "I hope you'll have enjoyed the voyage."

She hesitated ever so little. "Yes, much more than I expected."

"Did you think it would be very bad?"

"Horrible, horrible!"

The tone of these words was strange, but I hadn't much time to reflect upon it, for turning round at that moment I saw Jasper Nettlepoint come toward us. He was still distant by the expanse of the white deck, and I couldn't help taking him in from head to foot as he drew nearer. I don't know what rendered me on this occasion particularly sensitive to the impression, but it struck me that I saw him as I had never seen him before, saw him, thanks to the intense sea-light, inside and out, in his personal, his moral totality. It was a quick, a vivid revelation; if it only lasted a moment it had a simplifying certifying effect. He was intrinsically a pleasing apparition, with his handsome young face and that marked absence of any drop in his personal arrangements which, more than any one I've ever seen, he managed to exhibit on shipboard. He had none of the appearance of wearing out old clothes that usually prevails there, but dressed quite straight, as I heard some one say. This gave him an assured, almost a triumphant air, as of a young man who would come best out of any awkwardness. I expected to feel my companion's hand loosen itself on my arm, as an indication that now she must go to him, and I was almost surprised she didn't drop me. We stopped as we met and Jasper bade us a friendly good-morning. Of course the remark that we had another lovely day was already indicated, and it led him to exclaim, in the manner of one to whom criticism came easily, "Yes, but with this sort of thing consider what one of the others would do!"

"One of the other ships?"

"We should be there now, or at any rate tomorrow."

"Well then I'm glad it isn't one of the others" – and I smiled at the young lady on my arm. My words offered her a chance to say something appreciative, and gave him one even more; but neither Jasper nor Grace Mavis took advantage of the occasion. What they did do, I noticed, was to look at each other rather fixedly an instant; after which she turned her eyes silently to the sea. She made no movement and uttered no sound, contriving to give me the sense that she had all at once become perfectly passive, that she somehow declined responsibility. We remained standing there with Jasper in front of us, and if the contact of her arm didn't suggest I should give her up, neither did it intimate that we had better pass on. I had no idea of giving her up, albeit one of the things I seemed to read just then into Jasper's countenance was a fine implication that she was his property. His eyes met mine for a moment, and it was exactly as if he had said to me "I know what you think, but I don't care a rap." What I really thought was that he was selfish beyond the limits: that was the substance of my little revelation. Youth is almost always selfish, just as it is almost always conceited, and, after all, when it's combined with health and good parts, good looks and good spirits, it has a right to be, and I easily forgive it if it be really youth. Still it's a question of degree, and what stuck out of Jasper Nettlepoint – if, of course, one had the intelligence for it – was that his egotism had a hardness, his love of his own way an avidity. These elements were jaunty and prosperous, they were accustomed to prevail. He was fond, very fond, of women; they were necessary to him – that was in his type; but he wasn't in the least in love with Grace Mavis. Among the reflexions I quickly made this was the one that was most to the point. There was a degree of awkwardness, after a minute, in the way we were planted there, though the apprehension of it was doubtless not in the least with himself. To dissimulate my own share in it, at any rate, I asked him how his mother might be.

His answer was unexpected. "You had better go down and see."

"Not till Miss Mavis is tired of me."

She said nothing to this and I made her walk again. For some minutes she failed to speak; then, rather abruptly, she began: "I've seen you talking to that lady who sits at our table – the one who has so many children."

"Mrs. Peck? Oh yes, one has inevitably talked with Mrs. Peck."

"Do you know her very well?"

"Only as one knows people at sea. An acquaintance makes itself. It doesn't mean very much."

"She doesn't speak to me – she might if she wanted."

"That's just what she says of you – that you might speak to her."

"Oh if she's waiting for that!" said my companion with a laugh. Then she added: "She lives in our street, nearly opposite."

"Precisely. Thats the reason why she thinks you coy or haughty. She has seen you so often and seems to know so much about you."

"What does she know about me?"

"Ah you must ask her – I can't tell you!"

"I don't care what she knows," said my young lady. After a moment she went on: "She must have seen I ain't very sociable." And then, "What are you laughing at?" she asked.

"Well" – my amusement was difficult to explain – "you're not very sociable, and yet somehow you are. Mrs. Peck is, at any rate, and thought that ought to make it easy for you to enter into conversation with her."

"Oh I don't care for her conversation – I know what it amounts to." I made no reply – I scarcely knew what reply to make – and the girl went on: "I know what she thinks and I know what she says." Still I was silent, but the next moment I saw my discretion had been wasted, for Miss Mavis put to me straight: "Does she make out that she knows Mr. Porterfield?"

"No, she only claims she knows a lady who knows him."

"Yes, that's it – Mrs. Jeremie. Mrs. Jeremie's an idiot!" I wasn't in a position to controvert this, and presently my young lady said she would sit down. I left her in her chair – I saw that she preferred it – and wandered to a distance. A few minutes later I met Jasper again, and he stopped of his own accord to say: "We shall be in about six in the evening of our eleventh day – they promise it."

"If nothing happens, of course."

"Well, what's going to happen?"

"That's just what I'm wondering!" And I turned away and went below with the foolish but innocent satisfaction of thinking I had mystified him.

CHAPTER IV

"I don't know what to do, and you must help me," Mrs. Nettlepoint said to me, that evening, as soon as I looked in.

"I'll do what I can – but what's the matter?"

"She has been crying here and going on – she has quite upset me."

"Crying? She doesn't look like that."

"Exactly, and that's what startled me. She came in to see me this afternoon, as she has done before, and we talked of the weather and the run of the ship and the manners of the stewardess and other such trifles, and then suddenly, in the midst of it, as she sat there, on no visible pretext, she burst into tears. I asked her what ailed her and tried to comfort her, but she didn't explain; she said it was nothing, the effect of the sea, of the monotony, of the excitement, of leaving home. I asked her if it had anything to do with her prospects, with her marriage; whether she finds as this draws near that her heart isn't in it. I told her she mustn't be nervous, that I could enter into that – in short I said what I could. All she replied was that she IS nervous, very nervous, but that it was already over; and then she jumped up and kissed me and went away. Does she look as if she has been crying?" Mrs. Nettlepoint wound up.

"How can I tell, when she never quits that horrid veil? It's as if she were ashamed to show her face."

"She's keeping it for Liverpool. But I don't like such incidents," said Mrs. Nettlepoint. "I think I ought to go above."

"And is that where you want me to help you?"

"Oh with your arm and that sort of thing, yes. But I may have to look to you for something more. I feel as if something were going to happen."

"That's exactly what I said to Jasper this morning."

"And what did he say?"

"He only looked innocent – as if he thought I meant a fog or a storm."

"Heaven forbid – it isn't that! I shall never be good-natured again," Mrs. Nettlepoint went on; "never have a girl put on me that way. You always pay for it – there are always tiresome complications. What I'm afraid of is after we get there. She'll throw up her engagement; there will be dreadful scenes; I shall be mixed up with them and have to look after her and keep her with me. I shall have to stay there with her till she can be sent back, or even take her up to London. Do you see all that?"

I listened respectfully; after which I observed: "You're afraid of your son."

She also had a pause. "It depends on how you mean it."

"There are things you might say to him – and with your manner; because you have one, you know, when you choose."

"Very likely, but what's my manner to his? Besides, I HAVE said everything to him. That is I've said the great thing – that he's making her immensely talked about."

"And of course in answer to that he has asked you how you know, and you've told him you have it from me."

"I've had to tell him; and he says it's none of your business."

"I wish he'd say that," I remarked, "to my face."

"He'll do so perfectly if you give him a chance. That's where you can help me. Quarrel with him – he's rather good at a quarrel; and that will divert him and draw him off."

"Then I'm ready," I returned, "to discuss the matter with him for the rest of the voyage."

"Very well; I count on you. But he'll ask you, as he asks me, what the deuce you want him to do."

"To go to bed! – and I'm afraid" I laughed.

"Oh it isn't a joke."

I didn't want to be irritating, but I made my point. "That's exactly what I told you at first."

"Yes, but don't exult; I hate people who exult. Jasper asks of me," she went on, "why he should mind her being talked about if she doesn't mind it herself."

"I'll tell him why," I replied; and Mrs. Nettlepoint said she should be exceedingly obliged to me and repeated that she would indeed take the field.

I looked for Jasper above that same evening, but circumstances didn't favour my quest. I found him – that is I gathered he was again ensconced behind the lifeboat with Miss Mavis; but there was a needless violence in breaking into their communion, and I put off our interview till the next day. Then I took the first opportunity, at breakfast, to make sure of it. He was in the saloon when I went in and was preparing to leave the table; but I stopped him and asked if he would give me a quarter of an hour on deck a little later – there was something particular I wanted to say to him. He said "Oh yes, if you like" – with just a visible surprise, but I thought with plenty of assurance. When I had finished my breakfast I found him smoking on the forward-deck and I immediately began: "I'm going to say something you won't at all like; to ask you a question you'll probably denounce for impertinent."

"I certainly shall if I find it so," said Jasper Nettlepoint.

"Well, of course my warning has meant that I don't care if you do. I'm a good deal older than you and I'm a friend – of many years – of your mother. There's nothing I like less than to be meddlesome, but I think these things give me a certain right – a sort of privilege. Besides which my inquiry will speak for itself."

"Why so many damned preliminaries?" my young man asked through his smoke.

We looked into each other's eyes a moment. What indeed was his mother's manner – her best manner – compared with his? "Are you prepared to be responsible?"

"To you?"

"Dear no – to the young lady herself. I'm speaking of course of Miss Mavis."

"Ah yes, my mother tells me you have her greatly on your mind."

"So has your mother herself – now."

"She's so good as to say so – to oblige you."

"She'd oblige me a great deal more by reassuring me. I know perfectly of your knowing I've told her that Miss Mavis is greatly talked about."

"Yes, but what on earth does it matter?"

"It matters as a sign."

"A sign of what?"

"That she's in a false position."

Jasper puffed his cigar with his eyes on the horizon, and I had, a little unexpectedly, the sense of producing a certain effect on him. "I don't know whether it's YOUR business, what you're attempting to discuss but it really strikes me it's none of mine. What have I to do with the tattle with which a pack of old women console themselves for not being seasick?"

"Do you call it tattle that Miss Mavis is in love with you?"

"Drivelling."

"Then," I retorted, "you're very ungrateful. The tattle of a pack of old women has this importance, that she suspects, or she knows, it exists, and that decent girls are for the most part very sensitive to that sort of thing. To be prepared not to heed it in this case she must have a reason, and the reason must be the one I've taken the liberty to call your attention to."

"In love with me in six days, just like that?" – and he still looked away through narrowed eyelids.

"There's no accounting for tastes, and six days at sea are equivalent to sixty on land. I don't want to make you too proud. Of course if you recognise your responsibility it's all right and I've nothing to say."

"I don't see what you mean," he presently returned.

"Surely you ought to have thought of that by this time. She's engaged to be married, and the gentleman she's engaged to is to meet her at Liverpool. The whole ship knows it – though I didn't tell them! – and the whole ship's watching her. It's impertinent if you like, just as I am myself, but we make a little world here together and we can't blink its conditions. What I ask you is whether you're prepared to allow her to give up the gentleman I've just mentioned for your sake."

Jasper spoke in a moment as if he didn't understand. "For my sake?"

"To marry her if she breaks with him."

He turned his eyes from the horizon to my own, and I found a strange expression in them. "Has Miss Mavis commissioned you to go into that?"

"Not in the least."

"Well then, I don't quite see–!"

"It isn't as from another I make it. Let it come from yourself – TO yourself."

"Lord, you must think I lead myself a life!" he cried as in compassion for my simplicity. "That's a question the young lady may put to me any moment it pleases her."

"Let me then express the hope that she will. But what will you answer?"

"My dear sir, it seems to me that in spite of all the titles you've enumerated you've no reason to expect I'll tell you." He turned away, and I dedicated in perfect sincerity a deep sore sigh to the thought of our young woman. At this, under the impression of it, he faced me again and, looking at me from head to foot, demanded: "What is it you want me to do?"

"I put it to your mother that you ought to go to bed."

"You had better do that yourself!" he replied.

This time he walked off, and I reflected rather dolefully that the only clear result of my undertaking would probably have been to make it vivid to him that she was in love with him. Mrs. Nettlepoint came up as she had announced, but the day was half over: it was nearly three o'clock. She was accompanied by her son, who established her on deck, arranged her chair and her shawls, saw she was protected from sun and wind, and for an hour was very properly attentive. While this went on Grace Mavis was not visible, nor did she reappear during the whole afternoon. I hadn't observed that she had as yet been absent from the deck for so long a period. Jasper left his mother, but came back at intervals to see how she got on, and when she asked where Miss Mavis might be answered that he hadn't the least idea. I sat with my friend at her particular request: she told me she knew that if I didn't Mrs. Peck and Mrs. Gotch would make their approach, so that I must act as a watchdog. She was flurried and fatigued with her migration, and I think that Grace Mavis's choosing this occasion for retirement suggested to her a little that she had been made a fool of. She remarked that the girl's not being there showed her for the barbarian she only could be, and that she herself was really very good so to have put herself out; her charge was a mere bore: that was the end of it. I could see that my companion's advent quickened the speculative activity of the other ladies they watched her from the opposite side of the deck, keeping their eyes fixed on her very much as the man at the wheel kept his on the course of the ship. Mrs. Peck plainly had designs, and it was from this danger that Mrs. Nettlepoint averted her face.

"It's just as we said," she remarked to me as we sat there. "It's like the buckets in the well. When I come up everything else goes down."

"No, not at all everything else – since Jasper remains here."

"Remains? I don't see him."

"He comes and goes – it's the same thing."

"He goes more than he comes. But n'en parlons plus; I haven't gained anything. I don't admire the sea at all – what is it but a magnified water-tank? I shan't come up again."

"I've an idea she'll stay in her cabin now," I said. "She tells me she has one to herself." Mrs. Nettlepoint replied that she might do as she liked, and I repeated to her the little conversation I had had with Jasper.

She listened with interest, but "Marry her? Mercy!" she exclaimed. "I like the fine freedom with which you give my son away."

"You wouldn't accept that?"

"Why in the world should I?"

"Then I don't understand your position."

"Good heavens, I HAVE none! It isn't a position to be tired of the whole thing."

"You wouldn't accept it even in the case I put to him – that of her believing she had been encouraged to throw over poor Porterfield?"

"Not even – not even. Who can know what she believes?"

It brought me back to where we had started from. "Then you do exactly what I said you would – you show me a fine example of maternal immorality."

"Maternal fiddlesticks! It was she who began it."

"Then why did you come up today?" I asked.

"To keep you quiet."

Mrs. Nettlepoint's dinner was served on deck, but I went into the saloon. Jasper was there, but not Grace Mavis, as I had half-expected. I sought to learn from him what had become of her, if she were ill – he must have thought I had an odious pertinacity –

and he replied that he knew nothing whatever about her. Mrs. Peck talked to me – or tried to – of Mrs. Nettlepoint, expatiating on the great interest it had been to see her; only it was a pity she didn't seem more sociable. To this I made answer that she was to be excused on the score of health.

"You don't mean to say she's sick on this pond?"

"No, she's unwell in another way."

"I guess I know the way!" Mrs. Peck laughed. And then she added: "I suppose she came up to look after her pet."

"Her pet?" I set my face.

"Why Miss Mavis. We've talked enough about that."

"Quite enough. I don't know what that has had to do with it. Miss Mavis, so far as I've noticed, hasn't been above today."

"Oh it goes on all the same."

"It goes on?"

"Well, it's too late."

"Too late?"

"Well, you'll see. There'll be a row."

This wasn't comforting, but I didn't repeat it on deck. Mrs. Nettlepoint returned early to her cabin, professing herself infinitely spent. I didn't know what "went on," but Grace Mavis continued not to show. I looked in late, for a Goodnight to my friend, and learned from her that the girl hadn't been to her. She had sent the stewardess to her room for news, to see if she were ill and needed assistance, and the stewardess had come back with mere mention of her not being there. I went above after this; the night was not quite so fair and the deck almost empty. In a moment Jasper Nettlepoint and our young lady moved past me together. "I hope you're better!" I called after her; and she tossed me over her shoulder – "Oh yes, I had a headache; but the air now does me good!"

I went down again – I was the only person there but they, and I wanted not to seem to dog their steps – and, returning to Mrs. Nettlepoint's room, found (her door was open to the little passage) that she was still sitting up.

"She's all right!" I said. "She's on the deck with Jasper."

The good lady looked up at me from her book. "I didn't know you called that all right."

"Well, it's better than something else."

"Than what else?"

"Something I was a little afraid of." Mrs. Nettlepoint continued to look at me; she asked again what that might be. "I'll tell you when we're ashore," I said.

The next day I waited on her at the usual hour of my morning visit, and found her not a little distraught. "The scenes have begun," she said; "you know I told you I shouldn't get through without them! You made me nervous last night – I haven't the least idea what you meant; but you made me horribly nervous. She came in to see me an hour ago, and I had the courage to say to her: 'I don't know why I shouldn't tell you frankly that I've been scolding my son about you.' Of course she asked what I meant by that, and I let her know. 'It seems to me he drags you about the ship too much for a girl in your position. He has the air of not remembering that you belong to some one else. There's a want of taste and even a want of respect in it.' That brought on an outbreak: she became very violent."

"Do you mean indignant?"

"Yes, indignant, and above all flustered and excited – at my presuming to suppose her relations with my son not the very simplest in the world. I might scold him as much as I liked – that was between ourselves; but she didn't see why I should mention such matters to herself. Did I think she allowed him to treat her with disrespect? That idea wasn't much of a compliment to either of them! He had treated her better and been kinder to her than most other people – there were very few on the ship who hadn't been insulting. She should be glad enough when she got off it, to her own people, to some one whom nobody would have a right to speak of. What was there in her position that wasn't perfectly natural? what was the idea of making a fuss about her position? Did I mean that she took it too easily – that she didn't think as much as she ought about Mr. Porterfield? Didn't I believe she was attached to him – didn't I believe she was just counting the hours till she saw him? That would be the happiest moment of her life. It showed how little I knew her if I thought anything else."

"All that must have been rather fine – I should have liked to hear it," I said after quite hanging on my friend's lips. "And what did you reply?"

"Oh I grovelled; I assured her that I accused her – as regards my son – of nothing worse than an excess of good nature. She helped him to pass his time – he ought to be immensely obliged. Also that it would be a very happy moment for me too when I should hand her over to Mr. Porterfield."

"And will you come up today?"

"No indeed – I think she'll do beautifully now."

I heaved this time a sigh of relief. "All's well that ends well!"

Jasper spent that day a great deal of time with his mother. She had told me how much she had lacked hitherto proper opportunity to talk over with him their movements after disembarking. Everything changes a little the last two or three days of a voyage; the spell is broken and new combinations take place. Grace Mavis was neither on deck nor at dinner, and I drew Mrs. Peck's attention to the extreme propriety with which she now conducted herself. She had spent the day in meditation and judged it best to continue to meditate.

"Ah she's afraid," said my implacable neighbour.

"Afraid of what?"

"Well, that we'll tell tales when we get there."

"Whom do you mean by 'we'?"

"Well, there are plenty – on a ship like this."

"Then I think," I returned, "we won't."

"Maybe we won't have the chance," said the dreadful little woman.

"Oh at that moment" – I spoke from a full experience "universal geniality reigns."

Mrs. Peck however knew little of any such law. "I guess she's afraid all the same."

"So much the better!"

"Yes – so much the better!"

All the next day too the girl remained invisible, and Mrs. Nettlepoint told me she hadn't looked in. She herself had accordingly inquired by the stewardess if she might be received in Miss Mavis's own quarters, and the young lady had replied that they were littered up with things and unfit for visitors: she was packing a trunk over. Jasper made up for his devotion to his mother the day before by now spending a great deal of his time in the smoking-room. I wanted to say to him "This is much better," but I thought it wiser to hold my tongue. Indeed I had begun to feel the emotion of prospective arrival – the sense of the return to Europe always kept its intensity – and had thereby the less attention for other matters. It will doubtless appear to the critical reader that my expenditure of interest had been out of proportion to the vulgar appearances of which my story gives an account, but to this I can only reply that the event was to justify me. We sighted land, the dim yet rich coast of Ireland, about sunset, and I leaned on the bulwark and took it in. "It doesn't look like much, does it?" I heard a voice say, beside me; whereupon, turning, I found Grace Mavis at hand. Almost for the first time she had her veil up, and I thought her very pale.

"It will be more tomorrow," I said.

"Oh yes, a great deal more."

"The first sight of land, at sea, changes everything," I went on. "It always affects me as waking up from a dream. It's a return to reality."

For a moment she made me no response; then she said "It doesn't look very real yet."

"No, and meanwhile, this lovely evening, one can put it that the dream's still present."

She looked up at the sky, which had a brightness, though the light of the sun had left it and that of the stars hadn't begun. "It IS a lovely evening."

"Oh yes, with this we shall do."

She stood some moments more, while the growing dusk effaced the line of the land more rapidly than our progress made it distinct. She said nothing more, she only looked in front of her; but her very quietness prompted me to something suggestive of sympathy and service. It was difficult indeed to strike the right note – some things seemed too wide of the mark and others too importunate. At last, unexpectedly, she appeared to give me my chance. Irrelevantly, abruptly she broke out: "Didn't you tell me you knew Mr. Porterfield?"

"Dear me, yes – I used to see him. I've often wanted to speak to you of him."

She turned her face on me and in the deepened evening I imagined her more pale. "What good would that do?"

"Why it would be a pleasure," I replied rather foolishly.

"Do you mean for you?"

"Well, yes – call it that," I smiled.

"Did you know him so well?"

My smile became a laugh and I lost a little my confidence. "You're not easy to make speeches to."

"I hate speeches!" The words came from her lips with a force that surprised me; they were loud and hard. But before I had time to wonder she went on a little differently. "Shall you know him when you see him?"

"Perfectly, I think." Her manner was so strange that I had to notice it in some way, and I judged the best way was jocularly; so I added: "Shan't you?"

"Oh perhaps you'll point him out!" And she walked quickly away. As I looked after her there came to me a perverse, rather a provoking consciousness of having during the previous days, and especially in speaking to Jasper Nettlepoint, interfered with her situation in some degree to her loss. There was an odd pang for me in seeing her move about alone; I felt somehow responsible for it and asked myself why I couldn't have kept my hands off. I had seen Jasper in the smoking-room more than once that day, as I passed it, and half an hour before this had observed, through the open door, that he was there. He had been with her so much that without him she now struck one as bereaved and forsaken. This was really better, no doubt, but superficially it moved – and I admit with the last inconsequence one's pity. Mrs. Peck would doubtless have assured me that their separation was gammon: they didn't show together on deck and in the saloon, but they made it up elsewhere. The secret places on shipboard are not numerous; Mrs. Peck's "elsewhere" would have been vague, and I know not what licence her imagination took. It was distinct that Jasper had fallen off, but of course what had passed between them on this score wasn't so and could never be. Later on, through his mother, I had HIS version of that, but I may remark that I gave it no credit. Poor Mrs. Nettlepoint, on the other hand, was of course to give it all. I was almost capable, after the girl had left me, of going to my young man and saying: "After all, do return to her a little, just till we get in! It won't make any difference after we land." And I don't think it was the fear he would tell me I was an idiot that prevented me. At any rate the next time I passed the door of the smoking-room I saw he had left it. I paid my usual visit to Mrs. Nettlepoint that night, but I troubled her no further about Miss Mavis. She had made up her mind that everything was smooth and settled now, and it seemed to me I had worried her, and that she had worried herself, in sufficiency. I left her to enjoy the deepening foretaste of arrival, which had taken possession of her mind. Before turning in I went above and found more passengers on deck than I had ever seen so late. Jasper moved about among them alone, but I forbore to join him. The coast of Ireland had disappeared, but the night and the sea were perfect. On the way to my cabin, when I came down, I met the stewardess in one of the passages, and the idea entered my head to say to her: "Do you happen to know where Miss Mavis is?"

"Why she's in her room, sir, at this hour."

"Do you suppose I could speak to her?" It had come into my mind to ask her why she had wanted to know of me if I should recognise Mr. Porterfield.

"No sir," said the stewardess; "she has gone to bed."

"That's all right." And I followed the young lady's excellent example.

The next morning, while I dressed, the steward of my side of the ship came to me as usual to see what I wanted. But the first thing he said to, me was: "Rather a bad job, sir – a passenger missing." And while I took I scarce know what instant chill from it, "A lady, sir," he went on – "whom I think you knew. Poor Miss Mavis, sir."

"MISSING?" I cried – staring at him and horror-stricken.

"She's not on the ship. They can't find her."

"Then where to God is she?"

I recall his queer face. "Well sir, I suppose you know that as well as I."

"Do you mean she has jumped overboard?"

"Some time in the night, sir – on the quiet. But it's beyond every one, the way she escaped notice. They usually sees 'em, sir. It must have been about half-past two. Lord, but she was sharp, sir. She didn't so much as make a splash. They say she 'AD come against her will, sir."

I had dropped upon my sofa – I felt faint. The man went on, liking to talk as persons of his class do when they have something horrible to tell. She usually rang for the stewardess early, but this morning of course there had been no ring. The stewardess had gone in all the same about eight o'clock and found the cabin empty. That was about an hour previous. Her things were there in confusion – the things she usually wore when she went above. The stewardess thought she had been a bit odd the night before, but had waited a little and then gone back. Miss Mavis hadn't turned up – and she didn't turn up. The stewardess began to look for her – she hadn't been seen on deck or in the saloon. Besides, she wasn't dressed – not to show herself; all her clothes were in her room. There was another lady, an old lady, Mrs. Nettlepoint – I would know her – that she was sometimes with, but the stewardess had been with HER and knew Miss Mavis hadn't come near her that morning. She had spoken to HIM and they had taken a quiet look – they had hunted everywhere. A ship's a big place, but you did come to the end of it, and if a person wasn't there why there it was. In short an hour had passed and the young lady was not accounted for: from which I might judge if she ever would be. The watch couldn't account for her, but no doubt the fishes in the sea could – poor miserable pitiful lady! The stewardess and he had of course thought it their duty to speak at once to the Doctor, and the Doctor had spoken immediately to the Captain. The Captain didn't like it – they never did, but he'd try to keep it quiet – they always did.

By the time I succeeded in pulling myself together and getting on, after a fashion, the rest of my clothes I had learned that Mrs. Nettlepoint wouldn't yet have been told, unless the stewardess had broken it to her within the previous few minutes. Her son knew, the young gentleman on the other side of the ship – he had the other steward; my man had seen him come out of his cabin and rush above, just before he came in to me. He HAD gone above, my man was sure; he hadn't gone to the old lady's cabin. I catch again the sense of my dreadfully seeing something at that moment, catch the wild flash, under the steward's words, of Jasper Nettlepoint leaping, with a mad compunction in his young agility, over the side of the ship. I hasten to add, however, that no such incident was destined to contribute its horror to poor Grace Mavis's unwitnessed and unlighted tragic act. What followed was miserable enough, but I can only glance at it. When I got to Mrs. Nettlepoint's door she was there with a shawl about her; the stewardess had just told her and she was dashing out to come to me. I made her go back – I said I would go for Jasper. I went for him but I missed him, partly no doubt because it was really at first the Captain I was after. I found this personage and found him highly scandalised, but he gave me no hope that we were in error, and his displeasure, expressed with seamanlike strength, was a definite settlement of the question. From the deck, where I merely turned round and looked, I saw the light of another summer day, the coast of Ireland green and near and the sea of a more charming colour than it had shown at all. When I came below again Jasper had passed back; he had gone to his cabin and his mother had joined him there. He remained there till we reached Liverpool – I never saw him. His mother, after a little, at his request, left him alone. All the world went above to look at the land and chatter about our tragedy, but the poor lady spent the day, dismally enough, in her room. It seemed to me, the dreadful day, intolerably long; I was thinking so of vague, of inconceivable yet inevitable Porterfield, and of my having to face him somehow on the morrow. Now of course I knew why she had asked me if I should recognise him; she had delegated to me mentally a certain pleasant office. I gave Mrs. Peck and Mrs. Gotch a wide berth – I couldn't talk to them. I could, or at least I did a little, to Mrs. Nettlepoint, but with too many reserves for comfort on either side, since I quite felt how little it would now make for ease to mention Jasper to her. I was obliged to assume by my silence that he had

had nothing to do with what had happened; and of course I never really ascertained what he HAD had to do. The secret of what passed between him and the strange girl who would have sacrificed her marriage to him on so short an acquaintance remains shut up in his breast. His mother, I know, went to his door from time to time, but he refused her admission. That evening, to be human at a venture, I requested the steward to go in and ask him if he should care to see me, and the good man returned with an answer which he candidly transmitted. "Not in the least!" – Jasper apparently was almost as scandalised as the Captain.

At Liverpool, at the dock, when we had touched, twenty people came on board and I had already made out Mr. Porterfield at a distance. He was looking up at the side of the great vessel with disappointment written – for my strained eyes – in his face; disappointment at not seeing the woman he had so long awaited lean over it and wave her handkerchief to him. Every one was looking at him, every one but she – his identity flew about in a moment – and I wondered if it didn't strike him. He used to be gaunt and angular, but had grown almost fat and stooped a little. The interval between us diminished – he was on the plank and then on the deck with the jostling agents of the Customs; too soon for my equanimity. I met him instantly, however, to save him from exposure – laid my hand on him and drew him away, though I was sure he had no impression of having seen me before. It was not till afterwards that I thought this rather characteristically dull of him. I drew him far away – I was conscious of Mrs. Peck and Mrs. Gotch, looking at us as we passed – into the empty stale smoking-room: he remained speechless, and that struck me as like him. I had to speak first, he couldn't even relieve me by saying "Is anything the matter?" I broke ground by putting it, feebly, that she was ill. It was a dire moment.

Books For ALL Kinds of Readers

At ReadHowYouWant we understand that one size does not fit all types of readers. Our innovative, patent pending technology allows us to design new formats to make reading easier and more enjoyable for you. This helps improve your speed of reading and your comprehension. Our EasyRead printed books have been optimized to improve word recognition, ease eye tracking by adjusting word and line spacing as well as minimizing hyphenation. Our EasyRead SuperLarge editions have been developed to make reading easier and more accessible for vision-impaired readers. We offer Braille and DAISY formats of our books and all popular E-Book formats.

We are continually introducing new formats based upon research and reader preferences. Visit our web-site to see all of our formats and learn how you can Personalize our books for yourself or as gifts. Sign up to Become A RHYW Registered Reader.

www.readhowyouwant.com

Made in the USA
Monee, IL
07 July 2026